YAHWEH CALLS

Faith Stories for Young Children

Written by Judith Dunlap
Illustrated by Steve Erspamer, S.M.

ST. ANTHONY MESSENGER PRESS

Cincinnati, Ohio

D E D I C A T I O N

For the Church that raised me, especially:
my parents, Walter and Ann
my sisters, Joyce and Janice,
my grandparents, aunts and uncles,
as well as the Franciscans, Dominicans and Jesuits
who also taught me

———

Nihil Obstat: Rev. Nicholas Lohkamp, O.F.M.
Rev. Edward J. Gratsch
Imprimi Potest: Rev. John Bok, O.F.M.
Imprimatur: Most Reverend Carl K. Moeddel, V.G.
Archdiocese of Cincinnati, May 21, 1997

Illustrations by Steve Erspamer, S.M.
Cover and book design by Sanger & Eby Design
ISBN 0-86716-280-5
Text copyright ©1998, Judith Dunlap
Illustrations copyright ©1998, Steve Erspamer, S.M.
All rights reserved.
Published by St. Anthony Messenger Press
Printed in the U.S.A.

C O N T E N T S

Yahweh

There is only one God, but God has many names. One of God's names is Yahweh. God has been known as Yahweh for thousands of years. When you read the story of Moses you will find out how God got this name. In this book when we talk about God we will sometimes call God Yahweh.

In the Beginning

A long, long, long, long time ago, there were no trees, no flowers, no people, not even clouds or dirt. There was only Yahweh God. When Yahweh God called out, there was no answer. There was no thing or no one to call back. So Yahweh God made the heavens and the earth. Now when Yahweh called out, the land and the stars, the sun and the moon answered. Yahweh God saw that it was good.

Yahweh made the water rise out of the earth. The dirt became wet clay. Yahweh God took this clay and shaped it and reshaped it and made a man. Yahweh breathed into the man the breath of life. The man could walk and talk and sing and dance. When Yahweh God called out, the man answered, and God saw that he was good.

Yahweh made a great garden and filled it with all kinds of good things to eat. Yahweh God said to the man, "Eat and enjoy all that you like. There is only one thing to remember," Yahweh added. "Do not eat

from the tree in the middle of the garden. It is the tree of the knowledge of good and evil. If you eat from this tree, you will surely die."

Yahweh God saw the man walking and heard the man talking, but Yahweh did not see the man singing or dancing. Yahweh thought maybe the man was lonely. So Yahweh took some more clay and shaped all sorts of fish and animals and birds and insects.

God called out to each creature, big and small. Each creature answered. Yahweh saw that it was good.

The man loved all that Yahweh God had made, but still he did not dance and sing. Yahweh had an idea. When the man was asleep, God took one of his ribs and made a woman. Yahweh called out to the woman, and the woman answered. Yahweh saw that she was good.

When the man woke up, Yahweh brought the woman over to him. The man was so happy. "At last," he said, "I have a friend, a partner, someone like me." Yahweh God called out to both of them, and they began to sing and dance their answer.

The man's name was Adam and the woman's name was Eve. The man and woman were very happy. They had no chores to do. When they fell or bumped themselves, they did not get hurt. They never got colds or stomachaches. All of the animals in the garden were friendly. They could play with the lions and ride on the elephants. It was wonderful to live in the garden.

One day when the woman and the man were walking, they found themselves in the middle of the garden. In front of them was the tree of knowledge of good and evil. They remembered what Yahweh had told Adam. "Do not eat the fruit from this tree. If you do, you will surely die." The tree was beautiful. The fruit looked sweet and juicy. The man and the woman walked all around the tree. They stopped to look up through its branches.

While they were looking up, they heard a very small voice. The small voice said, "Go ahead, pick the fruit." The woman looked around, but she could not see anyone. "Go ahead, eat the fruit," the small voice said again. The man looked up and down, but he could not see anyone either.

"What's the matter?" the voice asked. "Did Yahweh God say you could not eat the fruit from the trees in

the garden?" The woman looked around again, and this time she saw a snake creeping out of the bushes.

"We can eat the fruit from any tree," the woman answered, "except this one. Yahweh God said we will surely die if we eat the fruit from this tree."

The serpent, who was very tricky, said, "Oh, that is not true. You will not die. Yahweh does not want you to eat this fruit because, if you do, you will become like gods."

The woman looked at the snake, and then she looked at the tree. The serpent said, "Look how ripe and juicy! I bet it is very sweet."

The tree was so beautiful and the fruit looked so good that the woman took a piece. She ate it, and then she gave it to the man. He ate it, too. Suddenly, they were filled with shame. When Yahweh God called to them, they hid.

"What have you done?" Yahweh asked. "Have you eaten the fruit I told you not to eat?"

The man answered, "The woman gave it to me." The woman said, "It is the serpent's fault." Yahweh God looked at the man and the woman. Yahweh said, "You ate the fruit you were told not to eat, and now you know good and evil. You must leave the garden.

From now on, you will have to work very hard. Sometimes you will get sick. When you fall down, you will get hurt. When you see a lion, you will have to run. And someday you will surely die."

Adam and Eve were sad to leave the garden. They were afraid, too. They knew things would never be the same—and they were right.

When they left the garden, they found many things to worry about. Sometimes they were hungry. Sometimes they were cold. They had to work very hard to find food and to make a safe place to live. Life had certainly changed for Adam and Eve.

There was only one thing that did not change when they left the garden. They were still very special to Yahweh God. God still loved them. Yahweh still called to them, and they called back. Even when they were cold and hungry, they sometimes sang and danced their answer. They knew how good it was to hear Yahweh call, and to know that Yahweh would be there no matter what happened.

And Yahweh God calls to us even today. *"I made you very special. I will always love you, no matter what."*

One Great God

There is one God. There will always be
One God who loves and looks after me.
God made whales and birds that sing.
One great God made everything.
God made me good. God made me free
To answer when God calls to me.

A Chosen People

Adam and Eve had many children. Their children lived all over the earth. As the years passed, the people forgot about Yahweh. They forgot that there was only one God. They began to pray to all sorts of gods. But Yahweh still called to them. Yahweh God chose a special people who heard the call. They were the Hebrew people. They would be Yahweh's special friends. In this book, you will meet some of these special friends who heard Yahweh's call.

Yahweh Calls Abraham and Sarah

A long, long, long time ago in a faraway land, there lived a man named Abraham and a woman named Sarah. Abraham and Sarah were husband and wife. They were very rich. They had many servants. They had a lot of animals. But Abraham and Sarah were not happy. They had many beautiful things, but they had no children. More than anything in the world, Abraham and Sarah wanted to have a child.

In the faraway land where Abraham and Sarah lived, the people prayed to many different gods. But Abraham prayed only to Yahweh. One day, Abraham heard Yahweh calling to him. This is what Yahweh said: "Abraham, I want you to leave this country. I want you to leave your friends and relatives. I want you to go to a land that I will show you. If you do this, I will make you a great nation. Your name will be famous."

Abraham and Sarah knew that they would miss their friends and relatives. They would miss their country. But they trusted Yahweh. Abraham especially liked the part where Yahweh said that he would become a great nation. This meant he and Sarah would have many children. Abraham and Sarah were very excited. They were eager to follow Yahweh's call.

So Abraham and Sarah left their country. They left with their nephew Lot. They took many servants. They needed them because they had many things to carry. They had many animals to care for.

They walked and they walked. After a while they camped out and rested. Then they packed up again and started walking. They had so many animals that they had to keep moving to find fresh grass for them to eat. This was how they lived.

They walked for days. They walked for months. They walked for years. Abraham became even richer. Every year he had more beautiful things to carry and more animals to take care of. But still Abraham and Sarah had no children. Abraham and Sarah would have traded all of their beautiful things to have a child.

Years and years passed. Abraham and Sarah grew older and older. Abraham thought that Yahweh had forgotten the promise that was made long ago. But Yahweh did not forget.

When Abraham was very old, Yahweh called to him again. Yahweh said, "You will become a great nation; you will have a son." Abraham fell down laughing because he thought he was too old to have children. Yahweh just kept on speaking, "You shall have children, and they shall have children. Look up in the sky and count the stars. That is how many great-great-great-grandchildren you will have."

Then Yahweh said to Abraham, "I am going to make a covenant with you." (A covenant is a very, very special promise.) "I have chosen you and all of your children and their children to be my special friends. You shall be my chosen people and I will be your God."

Abraham believed what Yahweh said, but this time he did not tell Sarah.

This is how Sarah found out she was going to have a son: One day, Abraham was sitting under a tree resting. He saw some men walking down the road. Abraham could see that they were special visitors. He ran up to them and asked them if they would please stop and rest for a while. He brought them cool water. He asked them to stay for dinner.

"Where is Sarah?" asked one of the men. "She is in the tent," answered Abraham. (He did not know that Sarah was standing by the tent door, listening to what they were saying.)

"When I come back next year," said the visitor, "Sarah will have a son." When Sarah heard this, she laughed out loud. "I am too old," she thought. The visitor heard Sarah laughing. He said to Abraham,

"Why is Sarah laughing? Doesn't she know that anything is possible for God?"

The strangers were messengers from God. They had come to let Sarah and Abraham know just how wonderful God was.

The messengers were right. The next year Sarah had her baby. Sarah and Abraham named the baby Isaac. *Isaac* means, "He laughed." It was a good name for the baby. Sarah and Abraham had both laughed when they heard they were going to have a child in their old age. And surely God must have laughed to see the Chosen People so happy.

God had called Abraham and Sarah, and they had answered. Now everyone was happy. They all laughed. And this is how God still calls to us today. *"I have chosen you. Trust in me. I keep my promises."*

Yahweh Calls Joseph

Along, long, long time ago, there lived a young boy named Joseph. Joseph was part of a large family. He had eleven brothers. Joseph's father loved all of his sons very much, but Joseph was his favorite. He had a special coat made for Joseph. It was a wonderful coat. It had long sleeves and many colors.

Some of Joseph's brothers did not like Joseph. They were jealous of him. They wanted to get rid of him. One day they saw some travelers walking down the road. One of the brothers pushed Joseph into a deep well. He said, "This is our chance. Let us sell Joseph to the travelers. They will take him far away."

"Good idea," said another brother, "but what will we tell our father? He will want to know why Joseph has not returned with us."

"I know what we can do," said a third brother. "I have an idea."

This was his idea: Before Joseph was taken away, the brothers tore off his wonderful coat. Then they killed a goat. They spilled some of the goat's blood on the coat. They took the coat back to their father and said, "Look what we found. It is Joseph's wonderful coat. It is all torn up, and it has blood on it. Some wild animal must have killed our brother." The father was very sad. He cried and cried.

Joseph was taken to Egypt. He was sold as a slave. He was treated very badly at first.

He was even locked up in jail. But Yahweh had given Joseph a special talent. Joseph could listen to people's dreams and tell what they meant.

One night, the king of Egypt had a bad dream. The dream made him afraid. The king thought that perhaps the dream was a message from God, but he did not know what the message was. The king had heard about Joseph's special talent. He called Joseph in to help him figure out the message.

Joseph listened to the king's dream. Joseph said, "You are right, God is giving you a message. God is telling you that for a few years there will be more than enough food for everyone. But in seven years, the crops will dry up. There will be no food to eat anywhere. God is giving you a warning," Joseph told the king. "You must put away enough food to feed all of the people for many years."

The king was grateful to Joseph for helping him see the warning. He put Joseph in charge of collecting the food. Joseph became a very important man. There was no one more important in all of Egypt, except the king.

God's warning came true. Very soon there was no food left. People began to come to Egypt to buy food so that they would not die. Joseph was in charge of selling the extra food. Anyone who wanted food had to come to Joseph.

Meanwhile, Joseph's brothers had all married. They had many children. When the crops in their country dried up, they had no food to eat. They decided to go to Egypt to buy some food.

When the brothers got to Egypt, they were taken to Joseph. They did not recognize him. He was all grown up. They knelt down in front of him and begged for food. At first, Joseph did not give them any. Instead he played a trick on them. He wanted to see if they were sorry for what they had done to him so many years ago.

Joseph told his servant to hide a silver cup in the bag of the youngest brother, Benjamin. A short time after the brothers had left the city, Joseph had his soldiers stop and search them. The soldiers found the cup and arrested Benjamin for stealing. They brought all of the brothers back to the city.

Joseph told the brothers that he was going to make a slave of Benjamin. When they heard this, they became very upset. The oldest brother went to Joseph and said, "Please make me a slave instead. Benjamin is the youngest of my father's sons. Years ago, our father lost

another young son, and it was our fault. If Benjamin does not return home, my father will cry and cry. We do not want to see our father so sad again. Please keep me instead."

Then Joseph told his brothers who he was. He said, "I am your brother, Joseph, whom you sold into slavery. Do not be afraid. I am not angry with you.

"As you can see, I am well. God has been with me. God has put me here so that I can take care of you. There will be many more years of hunger, but our family will not die. We are God's Chosen People."

Joseph was right. The famine went on for five more years. Many people died, but Joseph's family was safe. All of his brothers and all of their wives and all of their children lived well in Egypt. Joseph's father also came to Egypt. It was a happy day when Joseph and his father saw each other.

God called Joseph and Joseph answered. Even when things seemed very bad for Joseph, Yahweh made good things happen. Yahweh God took care of Joseph and Joseph took care of his family. And this is how God calls to us even today. *"I have chosen you. No matter how bad things may seem, I will take care of you."*

The Promised Land

Joseph and all of his brothers were Abraham's grandsons. Their children and their children's children were the Chosen People with whom God had made a special promise. Do you remember the special promise? It was called a covenant. Even though other people prayed to many gods, these people would pray only to Yahweh. Yahweh promised to always be with them.

Joseph and his brothers lived happily for many years. Their families grew and grew. Many, many years later, a new king came to rule Egypt. The new king did not like the Hebrew people, so he made them all slaves. Times got very hard for God's Chosen People, but they did not stop praying to Yahweh. And Yahweh did not leave them. Yahweh told them that they would be rescued. Yahweh promised them they would have a land of their own.

Yahweh Calls Moses

Along, long, long time ago, there lived a man named Moses. Moses lived in Egypt. He was a Hebrew, but he was not a slave like the other Hebrews. Moses was separated from his people when he was a baby. The king's daughter adopted him, and he was taken to the king's palace to live.

When Moses grew up he was lonely. He felt like he did not belong. Moses decided to leave the palace and find his own people. When Moses saw how badly they were treated, he felt very sorry for them.

Moses did not go back to the palace. Instead, he went to the country and helped to watch over some sheep.

One day Moses took the sheep to a far-off place. While he was there he saw something very strange. He saw a bush that was burning and burning, but it did not burn up. "I must go and see this strange sight," Moses said.

When he got closer, he heard a voice call out his name. "Moses, Moses!" the voice said. "Here I am," said Moses. "Come no nearer," said the voice. "Take off your shoes, Moses. This is holy ground. I am the God of your father, the God of Isaac, the God of Abraham," the voice said. Moses covered his face. He was afraid to look at God.

God said, "I have seen how badly my people are being treated. I hear their prayers to me. I am going to rescue them. I will give them their own land where they can live and be free. You are going to help me, Moses. You are going to lead my people. And when they are free, you will come back to this mountain and pray to me." Then God said, "I want you to go to the king and tell him to let my people go. You will lead them to freedom."

Moses told God that he did not think he could help. "I am a slow speaker. I can never think of the right things to say. I will never be able to talk to the king." God told Moses not to worry. He would find the words. God would be with him to make him strong and smart.

Before he left, Moses asked God what he should tell the people if they asked who had sent him. God said to Moses, "Tell them 'I AM' has sent me." In Hebrew, the word Yahweh means "I AM."

Yahweh also gave Moses special powers to convince the Hebrew people to follow him. With these powers and his strong words, Moses was able to talk the king into letting the people go. The young man who did not feel like he belonged had found his people and had become their leader.

Once the people had left Egypt, the king changed his mind. He sent his soldiers to catch the Hebrews and bring them back. The people came to a large sea. They did not know how they were going to cross it. They saw the soldiers coming. They thought they

were trapped. Then something wonderful happened. Yahweh separated the water so they could cross. When they were on the other side, the soldiers followed, but the water came together again. The soldiers were stuck, and the Chosen People went free.

Moses remembered what Yahweh had said. He took the people to the holy mountain where he had seen the burning bush. When they got there Moses climbed to the top. Yahweh spoke to Moses again. Yahweh gave Moses the Ten Commandments. These were the rules for the Chosen People.

The Chosen People walked for forty years before they settled in the Promised Land. Moses and the people had many great adventures on the way. Once when they had nothing to eat, Yahweh sent manna for them to eat. It tasted sweet. The people called it "bread from heaven."

Yahweh spoke to Moses many times, but Moses never forgot the first time Yahweh had spoken to him. Moses said yes to God, and God gave Moses what he needed to get the job done. And God speaks to us the same way today. *"You belong to me. When you walk with me, I will give you everything you need."*

Yahweh Calls Ruth

Along, long, long time ago, there lived a woman named Ruth. Ruth's husband was a Hebrew, but Ruth was not. They lived in a country called Moab. Ruth had lived all her life in Moab, but her husband and his family were from Judah. (Judah was part of the Promised Land.) Ruth's husband told her all about Yahweh and the Promised Land. "Someday," he told her, "we will go back to Judah, and we will make our home there."

Ruth's mother-in-law's name was Naomi. Naomi and Ruth worked together in the house. Naomi told Ruth stories about the Promised Land. She told Ruth about Abraham and Moses. She told Ruth about Yahweh's special promise to his Chosen People. Ruth dreamed about going to the Promised Land. She wanted very much to be with the Chosen People.

When Ruth was still young, her husband died. Her father-in-law and brother-in-law also died. It was very sad. Now there were no men left in the family.

Naomi decided that she was going to go back to the land of Judah. In Judah, she had family and friends who would help her. Ruth told Naomi that she would go with her. Naomi loved Ruth very much, but she told Ruth to go back to her own father's house. "I do not think you should go with me. I am old and poor. Your father is  rich. You are still young," Naomi said.

"You will meet someone else to marry, someone from your own land. You would be a stranger in Judah, and we would have nothing. It would be better for you if you went back to your father."

Ruth clung to Naomi. "Please," she said, "do not make me go back. I want to stay with you.

Wherever you go, I will go. Your land will be my land. Your people will be my people. Your God will be my God."

Naomi saw how determined Ruth was to stay with her. She saw how much Ruth wanted to go to the Promised Land. Naomi said no more. The two women went back to Judah. They went to Bethlehem, the city where Naomi had lived before she moved to Moab.

They had no money and no food. Ruth had to go out in the fields and gather up the leftover grain so that they would have food to eat. When she was out in the fields she was afraid that other people would make fun of her or hurt her because she was a foreigner.

One day she was gathering food in the field of a man named Boaz. Boaz had heard about Ruth. He knew how good she was to Naomi. He knew that she had stayed with Naomi and taken care of her. He also knew that Ruth wanted to make the Promised Land her home. He thought, "She is very brave. She is very loyal. She is a very special woman." Boaz told his servants to make sure no one made fun of Ruth and that no one hurt her. He also told his servants to leave extra grain for her to gather.

After a while things turned out very well for Ruth. Ruth and Boaz married. They had a son who they named Obed. Obed was the father of Jesse, and Jesse was the father of David. David was the greatest king that Judah would ever know.

Yahweh called Ruth through the stories of Naomi. Ruth listened to Yahweh's call. Ruth was loyal and faithful to the people she loved. She was also faithful to her dream. She had been a stranger in a strange land, but the Promised Land became her home. And this is how God still calls to us today.

"Listen, my children, you are all one family because you all belong to me. Take care of each other, as I take care of you. Be faithful to each other as I am faithful to you."

Kings and Queens

Over the years, the number of Hebrew people grew and grew. The land of Judah became a great nation called Israel. The people built beautiful cities and towns. They had wonderful farms and orchards. Jerusalem became the most important city. That is where Israel's greatest king had his court. In our first story, you will read about this great king. His name was David.

Some of the Chosen People moved to different countries and became rich and important. Even though they lived far from Israel, many of them kept the covenant. They did not forget Yahweh or Yahweh's special promise. They were faithful to Yahweh, and Yahweh was faithful to them. Our second story is about a Hebrew woman who lived in Persia. Her name is Esther. Esther became the queen of Persia.

Yahweh Calls David

A long, long, long time ago, there lived a boy named David. David lived with his father, Jesse, and his seven brothers. They lived in Bethlehem. David was the youngest in the family. It was his job to watch over the sheep. One day when he was in the fields with the flock, a wise man named Samuel came to town. Yahweh had told the wise man that the next king would be one of Jesse's sons. Yahweh had sent Samuel to bless the next king.

All of the people in the town gathered. They wanted to know why Samuel had come to town. Yahweh had told Samuel not to tell anyone why he was there. So Samuel told everyone he had come to worship with them. He invited Jesse and his sons to be with him when it was time to worship.

When Samuel saw Jesse's oldest son, he thought, "Surely this must be the next king. He is so fine-looking and so strong." But Yahweh said to Samuel, "He is not the one. God does not see as people see. People may care about what someone looks like on the

outside, but God looks at a person's heart." Samuel looked at each of Jesse's sons. He knew that the chosen one was not there.

Samuel asked Jesse, "Are these all of your sons?" Jesse said, "There is still the youngest. He is out in the fields with the sheep." Samuel told Jesse to send for him. When David came, he stood in front of Samuel. He was very young and small, but he had beautiful, gentle eyes. Yahweh said to Samuel, "This is the one. He is the one chosen to be the next king." Samuel took out the holy oils he had brought with him. He blessed David. From that day on the Spirit of Yahweh stayed with David.

David liked to look after the sheep. He took good care of them. Sometimes wild animals would come to steal from his flock, but David had a slingshot made out of a tree branch. He would shoot a stone from his sling and chase the animals away. David became very good with his sling.

One day his father came to David and said, "Three of your brothers have gone off to war. I am worried about them. I want you to go and take some extra food to them. I want you to find out how they are." David found someone to look after the sheep. Early the next morning, he left to find his brothers.

The Hebrew people were fighting a great war. The war was not going well. One of the enemy's soldiers was a giant of a man. His name was Goliath. Every morning Goliath would come out into the middle of the field. He would shout to the Hebrews, "Who will come out and fight me? We will settle this war with one fight. Choose a man. If he wins, your side will win the war. If I win the fight, our side wins the war." The Hebrews were afraid of Goliath. No one wanted to fight him.

David arrived at the camp just in time to hear Goliath call out to the soldiers. "Are you all cowards? Will no one come out to fight me?" When David heard Goliath say this, he told the soldiers, "I will fight him. I am not afraid." Everyone laughed. David was so small. He was just a boy. What could he do?

David went to the river and found five smooth stones. He put them in his pouch. Then he went to the field where Goliath was standing. David walked up to Goliath. Goliath looked at David and laughed. David said, "You are big and strong, but I have Yahweh on my side. You cannot win."

David took out one of the stones. He slung the

stone and hit Goliath right in the middle of his forehead. Goliath fell over. With one shot, David had won the fight. The war was over. The Hebrew soldiers all cheered. David was a hero.

David grew up to be a fine man. When the old king died, David became the new king. He was the best king the Hebrew people ever had.

David was chosen to be king when he was just a young man. God did not choose the oldest brother or the strongest. God chose David, and Samuel listened. God spoke to Samuel. God spoke to David. And God speaks to us the same way today. *"People may care about what someone looks like on the outside, but I look at a person's heart."*

Yahweh Calls Esther

Along, long, long time ago, there lived a beautiful Hebrew woman named Esther. Esther was not only beautiful on the outside, she was also beautiful on the inside. She had a good heart. She was kind and gentle. Esther lived in Persia, far from Israel. But Esther did not forget Yahweh. She was faithful to Yahweh and to Yahweh's commandments. Esther's mother and father had both died when she was very young. She lived with her uncle, Mordecai. She sewed for Mordecai and kept him company.

One day the king decided that he was going to marry. Mordecai thought that Esther would be a good wife for the king. He told Esther to dress up in her best clothes and to put perfume in her hair. Then Mordecai asked a friend to bring Esther to the king.

Just before she left, Mordecai warned Esther, "Do not let the king know that you are a Hebrew." Esther agreed. She knew that many people in Persia did not like the Hebrews.

When the king saw Esther, he thought she was the most beautiful woman he had ever seen. He also saw that Esther had a beautiful heart. The king married Esther and made her his queen.

Now there lived near the palace a man named Haman. Haman was very important. He was almost as important as the king. Haman was not a very nice man. He was very proud. He did not like Mordecai because Mordecai did not bow to the ground when Haman walked by him. When Haman told Mordecai to get on his knees, Mordecai said that he would only kneel to Yahweh.

Haman was very angry. He went to the king and told him a lie. He said the Hebrew people were going to make trouble for the king. Haman wrote out a paper that ordered all of the Hebrews to be killed. He tricked the king into signing the paper.

When Mordecai found out about the order, he sent a message to Esther. He told her go to the king. He said, "You must ask the king to change the order. You must ask him not to kill the Hebrew people."

Esther sent a message back to her uncle. She reminded him that she could not go to see the king. No one was allowed to see the king unless it was the king's idea. That was the law. "If I go without permission," she said, "the king will be very angry. He will tell the guards to kill me." Her uncle told her that she must try. She was their only hope.

Esther sent one more message to her uncle. "Ask all of the Chosen People to pray for three days. Then I will go and ask the king." So all of the Hebrew people prayed and prayed.

Esther also prayed to Yahweh. She prayed that Yahweh would give her courage. For three days she did not eat or drink anything. She only prayed. She became very weak from not eating any food.

Finally, at the end of the three days, she put on a beautiful gown and went to the king. When she entered the room where the king was, Esther had to lean on the arm of her servant. She was weak from fear and from hunger.

When the king saw Esther so weak, he was very worried. "What is it, my queen?" he said. "Ask for anything. Even if it is half of my kingdom, you shall have it." Esther answered, "My king, what I beg for is my life. I beg for the life of my uncle. I beg for the life of all of my people. I have always been loyal to you, and so have my people. Yet we are all ordered to die. I beg you to save us."

The king was very disturbed, "Who has ordered such a terrible thing? Who has ordered that you and your uncle and all of your people shall die?"

Esther answered, "Haman has ordered it. He tricked you into signing the paper." The king was very angry at Haman for lying to him. He called his guards and had Haman punished. Then he gave all of Haman's riches and property to Mordecai and Esther.

Esther was faithful to Yahweh. Yahweh was faithful to Esther. Esther prayed for courage so that she could speak to the king. Yahweh answered her prayer. And so God speaks to us even today. *"Come to me when you are afraid. I will comfort you. I will give you courage."*

Prophets and Heroes

Prophets were people who spent their lives listening for Yahweh's call. Prophets told the leaders and the Chosen People what Yahweh wanted them to do. Mostly the prophets reminded the people about the covenant, their special promise to pray to only Yahweh.

After a while, many of the Chosen People did not listen to the prophets. They forgot their promise to Yahweh. They broke the covenant, and they lost their land.

People from a country called Babylon became their rulers. They took many of the Hebrew people back with them to their own country. Some of the Hebrew people who were taken to Babylon remained faithful to Yahweh. Even though the people around them made fun of them or hurt them, they kept the covenant. They were heroes and heroines.

Yahweh Calls Elijah

A long, long, long time ago, there lived a man named Elijah. Elijah was a special friend of Yahweh. He was a prophet. Yahweh would give Elijah messages for the Chosen People. One day Yahweh had a special message for the rulers.

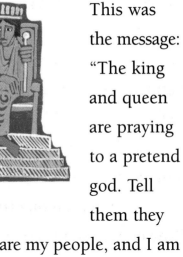

This was the message: "The king and queen are praying to a pretend god. Tell them they are my people, and I am their one and only God. They better not worship false gods."

Elijah told the king and queen that Yahweh did not like what they were doing. He told them they had better stop or there would be no rain for a long time. The rivers would dry up and there would be no water to drink. There would be no water to make their crops grow. Instead of listening to Elijah, the king and queen chased him out of town.

Sure enough, weeks and months went by and there was no rain. All the rivers dried up, and the crops did not grow. Instead of praying to Yahweh, the rulers and the Chosen People kept on praying to the pretend god. They blamed everything on Elijah because he was the one that told them it was going to happen. The king said, "If I ever see that Elijah again, I am going to kill him."

One day Yahweh spoke to Elijah. "Elijah, I want you to go to the king. Tell him that you will prove to him that I am the one true God. Tell him that soon Yahweh will send rain." Elijah said, "Yahweh, I cannot go to the king. He will kill me if he sees me." Yahweh answered, "Elijah, I will take care of you. I have a secret plan. Here is what I want you to do." Yahweh told Elijah the secret plan.

This was the plan: Elijah arranged a special contest with the prophets of the pretend god. Elijah told the

king to gather all of the prophets on a certain hill. Four hundred and fifty prophets came. Elijah called the Chosen People to the hill. He said to the prophets: "We will see who is the real God. You go ahead and pray to your god. Ask your god to make a great fire. You can pray all day if you want to. If the fire does not come, then it will be my turn to pray to Yahweh."

The four hundred and fifty prophets prayed and prayed. They danced their prayers. They sang their prayers. They shouted their prayers. They danced and sang and shouted from early morning until suppertime. They danced and sang and shouted until they could not move or speak any more. But nothing happened.

Finally, Elijah stood up. He said, "Now it is my turn." Elijah stepped forward and said in his everyday voice, "Yahweh, God of Abraham, God of Isaac, let your Chosen People know that you, Yahweh, are the one true God."

Suddenly there was a great flash. A huge fire lit the sky and flames filled the air. The people were very excited. "Yahweh is God!" they cried. "Yahweh is God!" Not long afterward it began to rain.

Yahweh won the contest. But still the king, the queen and many of the Chosen People prayed to the pretend god. The queen was really angry with Elijah. She sent a message to him. "Tomorrow I am going to kill you."

Elijah was really afraid. He ran away. He ran for a whole day. Finally, he sat down under a tree. He was tired and frightened. He was also very sad. He had done his best to call the Chosen People back to Yahweh. But he knew that most of them still prayed to the pretend god.

Elijah wanted to give up. He said, "Yahweh, I have had enough. Just let me die." But an angel came to him and said, "You'd better get up. You have a long walk ahead of you. You are to go to Yahweh's special mountain. When you get to the top, Yahweh will have a message for you." (This was the same mountain where Yahweh had talked to Moses.)

Elijah walked for forty days and forty nights. Finally he came to the mountain. He climbed to the top, and he waited. Suddenly there was a great wind. The wind was so strong that it made huge rocks break into pieces. But Yahweh was not in the wind. After the wind came a huge earthquake, but Yahweh was not in the earthquake. After the earthquake came a raging fire, but Yahweh was not in the fire. After the fire, everything became silent. And this is when Elijah heard Yahweh. He heard Yahweh in the quiet.

This is what Yahweh said to Elijah: "Everything will work out all right in my own time. Now you must go back. I have other work for you to do."

Elijah did what God asked, and everything did work out. The wicked queen died and the king stopped praying to the pretend god. Seven thousand of the Chosen People remained faithful to Yahweh. And everything worked out all right for Elijah.

Elijah learned a lesson. Sometimes we have to be quiet and still to hear God's voice. And Yahweh speaks to us the same way today. *"I am always with you. Even in the silence. Do not worry. Everything will work out in time."*

Yahweh Calls Daniel

A long, long, long time ago, there lived a young boy named Daniel. Daniel came from a good Hebrew family. Daniel lived during the time when Israel and Judah were no longer free. They were ruled by the king of Babylon. Many Hebrew families were forced to move to Babylon. Daniel's family was one of those families.

Daniel's family missed their homeland. They missed their old friends. But they did not miss Yahweh. They knew that Yahweh was still with them. The people of Babylon and many of the Chosen People prayed to all sorts of pretend gods. But Daniel's family was faithful to Yahweh. Each day they prayed three times to Yahweh.

Every year the king chose the smartest and strongest young people to come work in his palace. When Daniel was old enough, he was chosen. He studied and trained for years. When Daniel grew up he became a great leader in Babylon.

The other leaders were jealous of Daniel because he was the king's favorite. They decided they would find a way to get rid of him. They thought and they thought. Finally, they had an idea. They knew that Daniel prayed every day to Yahweh. They knew that he never missed a day. They decided that this was how they would trap Daniel.

The jealous leaders went to the king and said, "We think that you should tell everyone not to pray to any gods for thirty days. For thirty days people should only pray to you. In this way everyone will know how important you are."

"What a good idea!" said the king.

"Just to make sure everyone listens," the leaders continued, "we think you should sign an order that

says anyone who disobeys will be thrown into a lion's den."

"You are right," said the king. "This will make the people pay attention. I will sign this order." The leaders were excited. They had set a trap for Daniel.

Daniel heard about the new order. He knew that he would be punished if he prayed to Yahweh. But every day, three times a day he went to his house and prayed anyway. He opened the windows and knelt down. He faced his homeland and talked to Yahweh.

One day when he was in the middle of his prayers, the other leaders came running into his room. "We have caught you!" they said. "You know you are not supposed to pray to anyone but the king. Now you will be punished."

The king was very sad that he had to punish Daniel, but an order was an order. He had Daniel brought to him. He said to Daniel, "You are faithful to your God. May your God save you." Then he told his servants to throw Daniel into the pit where the lions were kept. They rolled some big rocks over the pit so that Daniel could not escape from the lions.

The lions were very hungry. They had not been fed for several days. They were ready to gobble Daniel up. But that is not what happened.

The next morning, bright and early, the king rushed over to the lion's den. "Daniel, Daniel," he cried. "Are you alive? Has your God saved you?" The king was very happy when he heard Daniel answer. "I am alive," Daniel said. "Yahweh sent an angel to close the lions' mouths so they could not hurt me." The king ordered the rocks to be taken away from the pit. Out walked Daniel without a mark on him.

Then the king sent out another order to all of the nations he ruled. This is what it said: "I order that the God of Daniel be honored and respected everywhere."

Daniel continued to serve the king and he also continued to serve Yahweh. Both the king and Yahweh knew who was most important to Daniel.

Yahweh speaks to us the same today. *"Come and talk to me. I like to spend time with you. When you are sad, or afraid, or lonely, come to me."*

The Promised Messiah

A long, long, long, long time ago, when Yahweh God called out in love, all of creation answered. The trees and flowers answered God's call by bending in the wind and lending the air the sweet smell of their blossoms and leaves. The sun, moon and stars answered God's call by shining brightly, making shadows and sunbeams. The creatures of the earth answered God's call by hooting and growling, croaking and snarling. And the people of the earth answered God's call by loving each other and loving God back. "This is good," said Yahweh God. "This is my Plan: everyone and everything in peace and harmony. This is how the world should be."

As time went by, things began to change. Sometimes Yahweh God would call out in love to the people and no answer would come back.

Sometimes, instead of loving each other and loving God, the people acted mean and selfish. Sometimes they even hurt each other. "This is not good," said Yahweh God. "This is certainly not my Plan."

So Yahweh chose a special people to help make the God Plan happen. Yahweh gave them some rules and their own Promised Land. Yahweh made a special promise: "I will never leave you. Stay close to me, and together we will make great things happen."

Sometimes the Chosen People stayed very close to Yahweh. Sometimes they did not. But there was always someone—a prophet, a king or queen, a hero

or heroine—who heard Yahweh's call and answered. Even when they lived far away from their homeland, some Chosen People stayed faithful. They never lost hope in Yahweh.

"I am still here," said Yahweh. "Remember, I will never leave you. Someday I will send you someone who will show you how to make the God Plan happen. I will send you an anointed one."

Yahweh God promised a Messiah. *Messiah* means "the anointed one." All through the hard times, the people waited and hoped and got ready for the coming of the Messiah.

We believe that Jesus was the promised one. We believe that he is the Messiah who came to show us how to make the Plan of God happen.

From the beginning of time, Yahweh God called out in love to all creation. Yahweh God calls out to us the same way today. *"If you hear my call, then love me with all your heart. I also want you to love each other as you love yourself. This is my Plan, that you love one another and live in peace and harmony."*

The Promised Messiah

Mighty one,
Emmanuel,
Servant,
Savior—
In God's time
Anointed
Herald of God's Plan.